Dear Parent:
Your child's love of reading starts here!

Every child learns to read in a different way and at his or her own speed. Some go back and forth between reading levels and read favorite books again and again. Others read through each level in order. You can help your young reader improve and become more confident by encouraging his or her own interests and abilities. From books your child reads with you to the first books he or she reads alone, there are I Can Read Books for every stage of reading:

SHARED READING
Basic language, word repetition, and whimsical illustrations, ideal for sharing with your emergent reader

BEGINNING READING
Short sentences, familiar words, and simple concepts for children eager to read on their own

READING WITH HELP
Engaging stories, longer sentences, and language play for developing readers

READING ALONE
Complex plots, challenging vocabulary, and high-interest topics for the independent reader

ADVANCED READING
Short paragraphs, chapters, and exciting themes for the perfect bridge to chapter books

I Can Read Books have introduced children to the joy of reading since 1957. Featuring award-winning authors and illustrators and a fabulous cast of beloved characters, I Can Read Books set the standard for beginning readers.

A lifetime of discovery begins with the magical words "I Can Read!"

Visit www.icanread.com for information
on enriching your child's reading experience.

for Lynn Klotz
who would certainly give
her little sister a Chompo Bar
if she had a little sister

I Can Read Book® is a trademark of HarperCollins Publishers.

A Birthday for Frances. Text copyright © 1968 by Russell Hoban. Illustrations copyright © 1968, 1995 by Lillian Hoban. Abridged edition copyright © 2012 Estate of Russell Hoban and Estate of Lillian Hoban. All rights reserved. Manufactured in China. No part of this book may be used or reproduced in any manner whatsoever without written permission except in the case of brief quotations embodied in critical articles and reviews. For information address HarperCollins Children's Books, a division of HarperCollins Publishers, 195 Broadway, New York, NY 10007.
www.icanread.com

Library of Congress Cataloging-in-Publication data is available.
ISBN 978-0-06-083795-2 (trade bdg.) — ISBN 978-0-06-083797-6 (pbk.)

20 SCP 10 9 8 7 ❖   First Edition

A BIRTHDAY
FOR FRANCES

by Russell Hoban
Pictures by Lillian Hoban

HARPER
An Imprint of HarperCollinsPublishers

It was the day before

Frances's little sister Gloria's birthday.

Mother and Gloria were making

place cards for the party.

Frances was in the closet, singing:

Happy Thursday to you,

Happy Thursday to you,

Happy Thursday, dear Alice,

Happy Thursday to you.

"Who is Alice?" asked Mother.

"Alice is somebody that nobody

can see," said Frances.

"That is why she has no birthday.

I am singing Happy Thursday to her."

9

"Today is Friday," said Mother.

"It is Thursday for Alice," said Frances.

"Alice will not have h-r-n-d."

"What is h-r-n-d?" asked Mother.

"Cake. I thought you could spell.

Alice will not have cake because

she does not have a birthday,"

said Frances.

"Alice has one birthday every year,

and so do you," said Mother.

"Your birthday is in two months.

Then you will be the birthday girl.

But tomorrow is Gloria's birthday."

"That is how it is, Alice," said Frances.

"Your birthday is always the one

that is not now."

"Wouldn't you and Alice like to come
out of the broom closet and help
me make place cards?" said Mother.
"What are you drawing?" Frances asked.
"Pretty flowers," said Gloria.
"Rainbows and happy trees."
Frances began to draw and sing:
A rainbow and a happy tree
Are not for Alice or for me.
I will draw three-legged cats.
And caterpillars with ugly hats.
Frances stopped singing.
"Gloria kicked me under the table,"
said Frances.
"Mean Frances," said Gloria.

"Gloria is mean," said Frances.

"Gloria hid my pail and my shovel."

"That was last year," said Mother.

"When Gloria is mean,
it was always last year," said Frances.

"But me and Alice know s-m-f-o."

"What is s-m-f-o?" asked Mother.

"Better," said Frances. "Good-bye.

I will be out of town visiting Alice."

Frances went to the broom closet

and took out her favorite broom.

"Let's go, Champ," she said.

"I'm ready to ride."

Frances was riding back and forth

on her broom on the porch, and as she

rode she sang a song for Alice:

Everybody makes a fuss

For birthday girls who are not us.

Girls who take your pail away

Eat cake and q-p-m all day.

"Is q-p-m ice cream?" Mother asked.

"Yes," said Frances.

Frances climbed up on one of
the porch rocking chairs
and looked through the window
at the boxes Mother was wrapping.
"What is Gloria getting from you
and from Father for her birthday?"
asked Frances.

"A paintbox and a tea set
and a plush pig," said Mother.
"I am not going to give Gloria
any present," said Frances.
"That is all right," said Mother,
and Frances began to cry.
"What is the matter?" said Mother.
"Everybody is giving Gloria
a present but me," said Frances.
"Would you like to give Gloria
a present?" said Mother.
"Yes," said Frances.

"If I had my next two allowances,
I would have a nickel and two pennies
and another nickel and two pennies,
and I could buy a Chompo Bar and
four balls of bubble gum for Gloria."

"I think it is very nice of you

to want to give Gloria

a birthday present," said Mother,

and she gave Frances

her next two allowances.

That evening Father took Frances

to the candy store

to buy a Chompo Bar

and four balls of bubble gum

for Gloria.

As they walked home

Frances said to Father,

"Are you sure that it is all right

for Gloria to have a whole Chompo Bar?

Maybe she is too young

for that kind of candy.

Maybe it will make her sick."

"Well," said Father, "I do not think

it would be good for Gloria to eat

Chompo Bars every day.

But tomorrow is her birthday,

and I think it will be

all right for her to eat one."

Frances thought about Gloria
and the Chompo Bar,
and while she thought she put two
of the bubble-gum balls into her mouth
without noticing it.

Frances chewed the bubble gum
and squeezed the Chompo Bar a little.
"Chompo Bars have nougat, caramel,
chocolate, and nuts," said Frances.

"Probably Gloria could not eat
more than half of one."
"I'm sure that Gloria could eat
the whole Chompo Bar," said Father.
"That is why it is such a good present."
"Yes," said Frances,
"and I spent two allowances on Gloria."
Frances put the other two gum balls
into her mouth and sang:
Chompo Bars are nice to get.
Chompo Bars taste better yet
When they're someone else's.
"You would not eat Gloria's Chompo Bar,
would you?" said Father.
"It is not Gloria's yet," said Frances.

"I can hardly understand

what you are saying," said Father.

"Is there something in your mouth?"

"I think maybe there is bubble gum,"

said Frances, "but I don't remember

how it got there."

"Maybe I should take care of

the Chompo Bar until you are ready

to give it to Gloria," said Father.

"All right," said Frances,

and she gave the Chompo Bar

to Father to take care of.

The next day was Gloria's birthday,
and the party was that afternoon.

The cake was ready,

the table was all set,

and Mother was making hot chocolate.

There were little baskets of gum drops

and chocolate-covered peanuts

for everybody.

There were place cards

and party poppers

for Mother and Father,

for Frances and Gloria,

for Gloria's friend Ida,

and for Frances's friend Albert.

Albert was the first friend to arrive,

and he and Frances sat down

while they were waiting for Ida.

"What are you giving Gloria?"

Frances asked Albert.

"A little tiny truck," said Albert.

30

"I am thinking of giving Gloria

a Chompo Bar," said Frances.

"But I am not sure.

I might and I might not.

I had to spend almost two

whole allowances on it."

"That's how it is," said Albert.

"I had to spend my allowance money

on my sister when she had a birthday."

"Little sisters are not much r-v-s-m,"

said Frances.

"Good?" said Albert.

"That's right," said Frances.

"No, they are not," said Albert.

"Little sisters can't catch
or throw," said Albert.
"They take your sand pail
and your shovel too," said Frances.

"I don't think many of them deserve

a Chompo Bar."

"Here is Ida now," said Mother,

"and the party can begin."

"When are the presents?" said Gloria.

"First," said Father, "your mother
will bring out the cake,
and I will light the candles.
We will sing 'Happy Birthday to You.'
Then you make a wish.
Then you get your presents."

"I know what to wish," said Gloria.

"Don't tell it," said Ida.

"It won't come true if you do,"

said Albert.

"Here comes the cake," said Mother.

She put it on the table,

and Father lit the candles.

Then everybody sang

"Happy Birthday to You."

Frances did not sing the words
that the others were singing.
Very softly, so that nobody
could hear her, she sang:
Happy Chompo to me
Is how it ought to be—
Happy Chompo to Frances,
Happy Chompo to me.
"Make your wish and blow out
the candles," said Mother to Gloria.
"I want to tell my wish," said Gloria.
"No, no!" said Mother and Father
and Frances and Albert and Ida.

"Just say it inside your head,"
said Albert.
Gloria said her wish inside her head
and blew out the candles at once.
"Hooray!" said everybody.

"Now your wish will come true,"
said Mother.

"This is what I wished," said Gloria:
"I wished that Frances would be nice
and not be mad at me
because I hid her sand pail
and shovel last year.
And I am sorry, and I will be nice."

"She told," said Ida.

"Now her wish won't come true."

"I think it will come true,"
said Mother, "because it is
a special kind of good wish
that can make itself come true."

39

"Well," said Frances to Gloria,

"I think your wish will come true too.

And I have a present for you,

and I owe you four balls

of bubble gum."

"Now it is time for the presents?"

said Gloria.

"Yes," said Father.

Father and Mother gave Gloria

the paintbox and the tea set

and the plush pig.

Albert gave her the little tiny truck.

Ida gave her a little china baby doll.

Frances had wrapped the Chompo Bar

in pretty paper

and tied it with a ribbon,

and now she got ready to give it to Gloria.

"What is it?" asked Gloria.

"It is something good to eat,"
said Frances,

"and I will give it to you in a minute.

But first I will sing

'Happy Birthday to You,'

because I did not really sing it before.

Happy birthday to you," sang Frances,

and she squeezed the Chompo Bar.

"Happy birthday to you."

Then she stopped
and rested a little.

"You can have a bite when I get it,"
said Gloria.

Frances took a deep breath

and finished the song,

"Happy birthday, dear Gloria,

happy birthday to you.

Here," said Frances.

She squeezed the Chompo Bar

one last time and gave it to Gloria.

"You can eat it all, because

you are the birthday girl," said Frances.

"Thank you," said Gloria

as she unwrapped the Chompo Bar.

"This is a good present."

And she ate it all,

because she was the birthday girl.